THIS BOOK BELONGS TO

FOR EDDIE AND BILL WITH LOVE — P.F.

TO DENISE AND LOUISE — R.J.

First published 2022 by Walker Books Ltd, 87 Vauxhall Walk, London SE11 5HJ

2 4 6 8 10 9 7 5 3 1

Text © 2022 Polly Faber
Illustrations © 2022 Richard Jones

This book has been typeset in Chaparral Pro

Printed in China

British Library Cataloguing in Publication Data: a catalogue record for this book is available from the British Library

ISBN 978-1-4063-9767-3

www.walker.co.uk

WALKER BOOKS
AND SUBSIDIARIES
LONDON · BOSTON · SYDNEY · AUCKLAND

Through the North Pole Snow

POLLY FABER ILLUSTRATED BY RICHARD JONES

A little fox came hunting through the snow.

She was trying to find something – anything – for her dinner.

Everywhere was so cold.

Everywhere was so dark.

Hop! Hop!

Thump!

Again and again, she sprang up and
punched down into the thick white blanket.

Some places the ground was too hard and the snow too shallow.

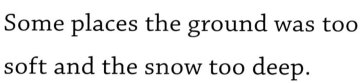

Some places the ground was too soft and the snow too deep.

But, in one place...

Ah!

The little fox saw light and colour

and felt warmth again.

And the little fox smelled dinner.

She
scrabbled and
wriggled
and
wriggled
and
scrabbled.

But the little fox could

not get through.

"Stuck? Now that's a problem I understand!"

Two hands took hold
of the little fox
and pulled.

The hands belonged to a man with a great round belly and a fox-white beard. He looked very old and very tired but so kind that the little fox couldn't be frightened.

"Help yourself to dinner. There's plenty left over; I was already full of cookies," the old man said, and he gave a yawn and went to bed.

By the light of the giant log glowing
on the fire, the little fox explored.

There were snowy boots and steaming clothes.
There were piles of paper everywhere.
And there were rows and rows of empty shelves.

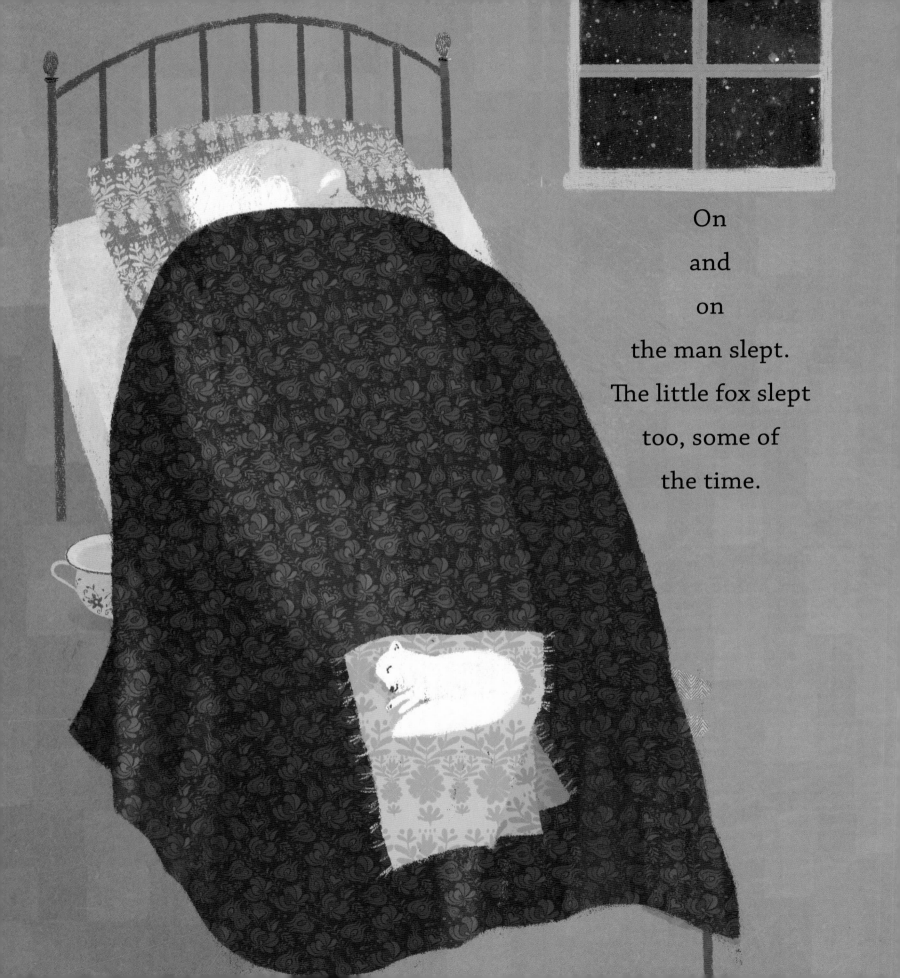

On
and
on
the man slept.
The little fox slept
too, some of
the time.

Until one day a shaft of sunlight shone through
the hole in the ceiling, and the man sat up with a stretch.
He smiled when he saw the little fox: "You still here?"
He didn't look so old now.

With the world lit bright again,
the little fox played outside and found flowers.
She chased insects and followed streams.

Sometimes
the man came too
but mostly now
he was busy.

He drew and measured and made plans.

He sawed and painted and hammered.

And he cut and sewed and stuffed.

And slowly,

slowly,

he filled up all the empty shelves from their tops

to their bottoms.

When the sun began to sink away once more
and the first snow arrived, something else fell with it:
letters. They floated through the sky. Hundreds,
then thousands of them.

The little fox helped the man find every single one.

Then the man read and he read.

He made lists.

He matched lists to his shelves with notes,

with addings and crossings.

And he filled a great sack. He didn't stop until ...

... coloured lights came dancing across the sky and eight reindeer arrived.
Pawing and snorting and steaming, they dipped their heads for silver
bells to be tied to their antlers and were harnessed to a sleigh.

"Coming, little fox?" asked the man.

His eyes sparkled brighter than snow.

The little fox came.

And finally, she understood everything.

And when the sleigh was empty,
the fox found her heart was full.

And together, the fox and Father Christmas came home.